vampenguin

by LUCY RUTH CUMMINS

ZOO

A
atheneum

Atheneum Books for Young Readers

NEW YORK   LONDON   TORONTO   SYDNEY   NEW DELHI

For Siobhan

The author would like to gratefully acknowledge and thank the Spruceton Inn Artist Residency program for allowing her time and space necessary to dream up this story.

ATHENEUM BOOKS FOR YOUNG READERS

An imprint of Simon & Schuster Children's Publishing Division

1230 Avenue of the Americas, New York, New York 10020

© 2021 by Lucy Ruth Cummins

Book design by Sonia Chaghatzbanian and Lucy Ruth Cummins © 2021 by Simon & Schuster, Inc.

ATHENEUM BOOKS FOR YOUNG READERS is a registered trademark of Simon & Schuster, Inc.

Atheneum logo is a trademark of Simon & Schuster, Inc.

For information about special discounts for bulk purchases, please contact Simon & Schuster Special Sales at 1-866-506-1949 or business@simonandschuster.com.

The Simon & Schuster Speakers Bureau can bring authors to your live event. For more information or to book an event, contact the Simon & Schuster Speakers Bureau at 1-866-248-3049 or visit our website at www.simonspeakers.com.

The text for this book was set in Bodoni 72.

The illustrations for this book were rendered in gouache and colored pencil, and finished with digital line.

Manufactured in China

0421 SCP

First Edition

2 4 6 8 10 9 7 5 3 1

Library of Congress Cataloging-in-Publication Data

Names: Cummins, Lucy Ruth, author, illustrator.

Title: Vampenguin / Lucy Ruth Cummins.

Description: First edition. | New York : Atheneum Books for Young Readers, [2021] | Audience: Ages 4–8. | Audience: Grades K–1. | Summary: A young vampire trades places with a penguin at the zoo for a day of mischief and fun.

Identifiers: LCCN 2020022078 (print) | LCCN 2020022079 (eBook) | ISBN 9781534466982 (hardcover) | ISBN 9781534466999 (eBook)

Subjects: CYAC: Vampires—Fiction. | Penguins—Fiction. | Zoos—Fiction.

Classification: LCC PZ7.1.C86 Vam 2021 (print) | LCC PZ7.1.C86 (eBook) | DDC [E]—dc23

LC record available at https://lccn.loc.gov/2020022078

LC ebook record available at https://lccn.loc.gov/2020022079

On Saturday, the Dracula family woke up extra early
so they could beat the weekend crowds to the zoo.

After a short wait in line, they made their way through the turnstiles.

Their first stop was always the Penguin House.

The room was chilly, dark, and full of visitors.

There were Adélie penguins,
African penguins, chinstraps,
flashy southern rockhoppers, and
even a handful of emperor penguins.

After they'd seen everything there was to see,
they were ready for something different.

Back in the penguin enclosure, it was time for breakfast.

There was *almost*
enough to go around.

Outdoors, the Draculas first saw the tiger;

then the elephants;

then the monkeys;

and finally, the lion.

At the bear exhibit, the Draculas argued back and forth about if it was a grizzly or a brown bear.

The only thing they *could* agree on was that it was majestic.

There was a lot to take in.

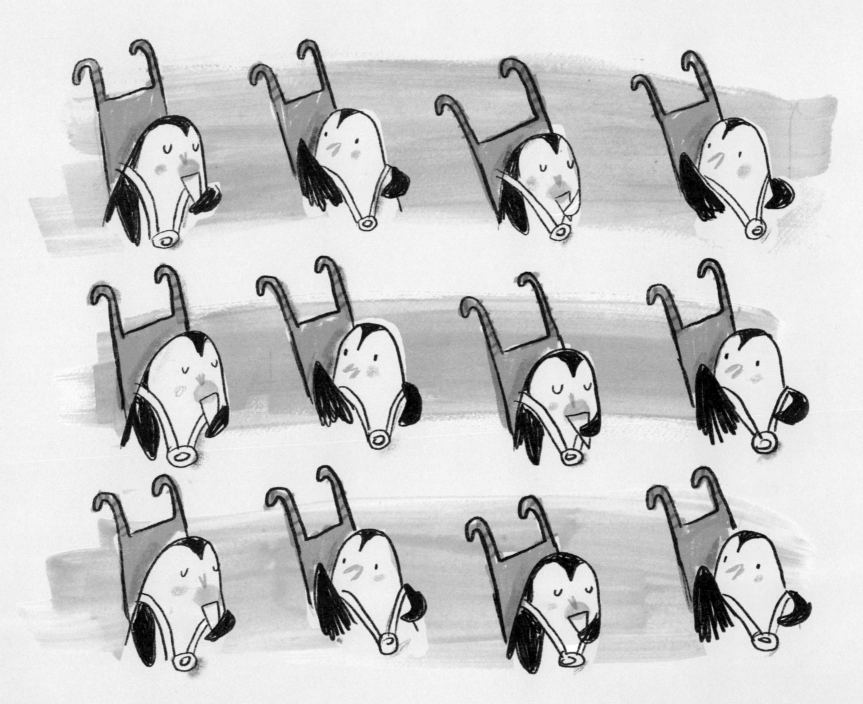

After they had their fill,

the Draculas made their way to the aviary.

They flew right through it.

Back outside, the entire Dracula family was absolutely *delighted* by the sea lion behavior demonstration.

And back at the
Penguin House . . .

First, one penguin
made a splash . . .

and another one made an even bigger splash.

On the opposite side of the zoo, the Draculas ran into some old friends.

At the penguin exhibit, some respectful children
came to quietly observe the penguins.

For some reason
they didn't hang around.

It was getting late, and the last stop for the Draculas was the polar bear exhibit. They knew they had to get moving if they wanted to beat the evening rush home.

At the same time, across the zoo in another cold room, the penguin
exhibit was suddenly proving to be a treat for all the senses.

On their way to the exit, the Dracula family happily posed for a souvenir picture.

And Junior insisted they stop for a balloon in his favorite color.

Off they went!

The Draculas would never
forget their visit to the zoo . . .

and neither would the penguins.

THE END